ZIGBY ™
CAMPS OUT

BRIAN PATERSON

HarperCollins *Children's Books*

For William, Charles and Henry

First published in Great Britain by HarperCollins Publishers Ltd in 2002

1 3 5 7 9 10 8 6 4 2

ISBN: 978-0-00-780274-6

Text copyright © Alan MacDonald, Brian and Cynthia Paterson and HarperCollins Publishers Ltd 2002
Illustrations copyright © Brian Paterson 2002

Text by Alan MacDonald

ZIGBY™ and the Zigby character logo are trademarks of HarperCollins Publishers Ltd.

The authors and illustrator assert the moral right to
be identified as the authors and illustrator of the work.
A CIP catalogue record for this title is available from the British Library.

The HarperCollins website address is: www.fireandwater.com

Printed and bound in Malaysia by Imago

Follow the winding stream to the
edge of the jungly forest and meet...

ZIGBY THE ZEBRA
OF MUDWATER CREEK.

Zigby the Zebra loves being outdoors, getting up
to mischief with his good friends, Bertie and McMeer.
There are always exciting new places to explore
and wonderful adventures waiting to happen
but sometimes he can't help trotting
straight into trouble!

Meet his friend, the African guinea fowl, Bertie Bird.
He's easily scared and thinks his friends are far too
naughty...but he'd hate to miss the fun, even if it does
mean getting dirty feathers!

McMeer is the cheeky little meerkat who
loves showing off and playing tricks. His practical
jokes sometimes cause all sorts of problems,
but he always knows how to have fun!

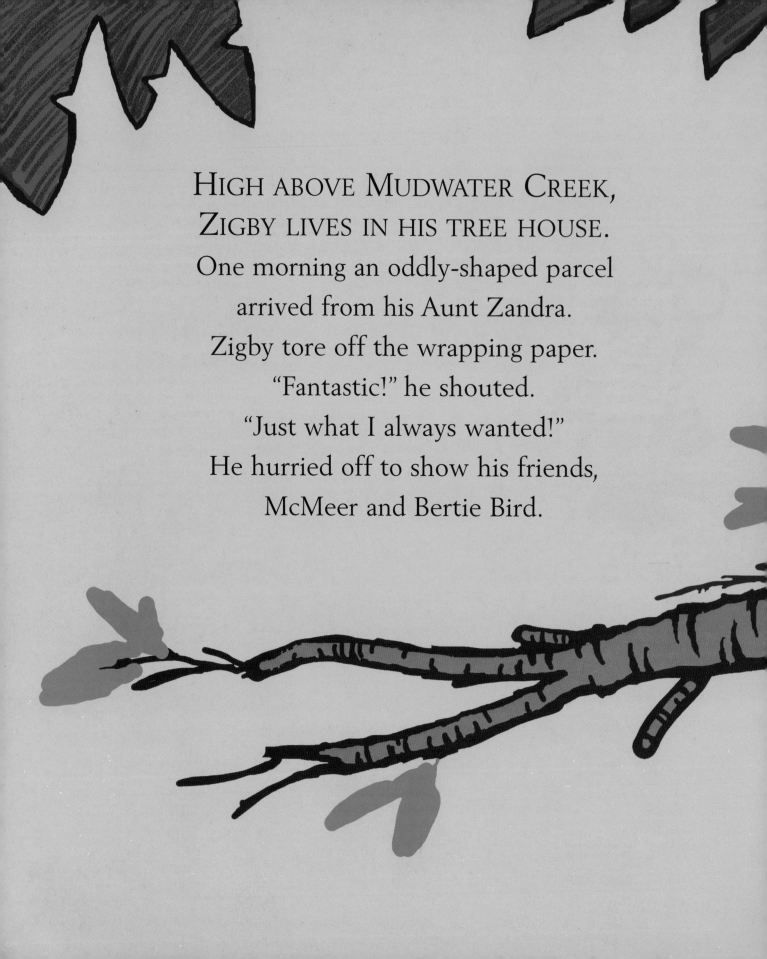

HIGH ABOVE MUDWATER CREEK,
ZIGBY LIVES IN HIS TREE HOUSE.
One morning an oddly-shaped parcel
arrived from his Aunt Zandra.
Zigby tore off the wrapping paper.
"Fantastic!" he shouted.
"Just what I always wanted!"
He hurried off to show his friends,
McMeer and Bertie Bird.

McMeer sniffed the lumpy shape.
"Is it a sausage?" he asked, hopefully.

"Don't be silly," laughed Zigby. "It's a tent. Now we can all go camping!"

McMeer rolled head over heels. He'd never been camping before. Neither had Bertie, who hoped it wasn't too dangerous.

The friends set out on their big adventure.
Zigby picked up a swishy stick in case they met
anything frightening.
"Where are you three going?" asked Ella the elephant.
"We're going to camp in the darkest jungle," said Zigby.
"Better take a watermelon," advised Ella. "Camping is
hungry work."

"Let's camp here," Zigby suggested.
The tent proved rather a puzzle. There were so many poles and pegs.
"It's a bit wonky but it will do," said McMeer.
The three friends squashed into the tent.

"This is fun!" said Zigby.
"When do we eat?" asked Bertie.
McMeer thought that they should make a fire first.
"You two wait here while I go and fetch
some wood," he said.

Zigby and Bertie waited in the tent for McMeer to come back. The sun sank slowly below the trees and the jungle began to get dark. Outside the forest was alive with strange sounds. Bertie moved closer to Zigby.

"What's that noise?" he whispered.

"What noise?" asked Zigby.

"That something-lurking-in-the-dark noise," said Bertie. Zigby listened and he heard it too.

Nervously he felt for his swishy stick.

Bertie moved even closer to Zigby.
"What's *that* noise?" he whispered.
"What noise?" asked Zigby.

"That something-waiting-to-pounce noise," said Bertie.
Zigby listened and he heard it too...a rustling, scuffling
sound...coming nearer.

Suddenly Bertie clung to Zigby, trembling.
"It's right outside!" he said. "I can hear
it dribbling and snarling."
"I hear it, too," said Zigby, "and

THERE IT IS!"

A tall shadow loomed
over them. Bravely, Zigby
poked it through the
side of the tent with
his swishy stick.

"It's McMeer!" cried Zigby.
They went outside and found McMeer
slurping the last mouthful of watermelon.
"Did I scare you?" giggled McMeer.

For playing tricks on them,
McMeer had to stay outside
and build the fire all by himself.
"And you're not coming in
until it's finished," said Zigby,
closing the tent flap.

McMeer put a last stick on the fire. Then he pricked up his ears. From somewhere in the forest came a sound like distant thunder.

It was coming towards them…

...growing louder and

LOUDER.

It made the ground shake and the trees tremble.

McMeer shook the tent.

"Let me in! Let me in!" he begged.

"There's something coming!"

"McMeer, we know it's you. Stop playing games,"
answered Zigby.

"No! Don't leave me out here, please!" wailed McMeer.
"Can't you hear it?"
Zigby and Bertie listened. The rumbling, thundering
noise was very close now.
Bertie opened the tent flap and McMeer dived inside.
The three friends huddled together in the dark, hardly
daring to breathe.

"THUMP,

 THUMP,

THUMP,"

…came the noise outside.

Suddenly the tent flap was pulled back by something
long and snake-like...

"Hello!" said a friendly face. "I just came to say good night. Are you having a good time?"
"No! We're cold and hungry," said Bertie, "and McMeer ate all the watermelon."
"Well, why don't you come home?" asked Ella. "I've just been making some supper."

After the biggest supper they'd ever eaten,
everyone was ready for bed.
"What about your tent?" asked Ella.
"It seems a shame to pack it away."
"I know just the place for it," said Zigby.

Good night, Zigby. Sweet dreams!